Nikolai Vasilevich Gogol was born on [   ]

Ukraine. In December 1828 he moved [   ] ....u in

one government ministry, and then another; and after abandoning these

two jobs he tried and failed to become an actor. He wrote *Hanz*

Kuechelgarten and published it at his own expense. It was reviewed in the

Moscow Telegraph and the *Northern Bee*, and then Gogol bought all the

copies he could find of his book and burnt them. He left the country

and returned and re-entered the civil service. In March 1830 *Fatherland*

Notes published one of his Ukrainian tales; and eight more stories

appeared over the following two years. They made Gogol famous.

Baron Delvig, editor of *Northern Flowers*, introduced him to Pushkin. In

the following years Gogol started to write about St. Petersburg, and

published, *The Diary of a Madman, Nevsky Prospect* and *The Nose*, amongst

other stories; and his most famous play, *The Government Inspector*, had its

premier; and he wrote the early drafts of *Marriage*. And Gogol was at the

top of his fame in June 1836 when he left Russia for Switzerland, Paris

and Rome. In Rome he wrote the first volume of *Dead Souls* – his only

novel. He returned to St. Petersburg, and then to Rome, where he wrote

The Overcoat in October 1841. Then he returned again to St Petersburg,

and in 1842 he published *Dead Souls*, and a four volume collection of

short stories and plays. After which he became increasingly religious and

increasingly restless. His travels took him as far as Palestine – as a

pilgrim. He wrote the second volume of *Dead Souls*, but this went the

same way as *Hanz Kuechelgarten* – he burnt it. He fasted to the point of

exhaustion, and doctors purged him and bled him with leeches, and he

died on 4th March, 1852, at the age of 43.

Gogol received the appropriate punishment for his bad conduct... Gogol placed in the corner on account of indecent expressions... Gogol in the corner for uncleanliness... Gogol without tea for stubbornness and very extraordinary laziness... Gogol playing with toys in the religious class – deprived of tea.

School report, 1824

Petersburg is not what I expected – I had imagined it would be much more beautiful and magnificent. It seems people have been spreading false rumours about it. It is an amazingly quiet place; the people seem more dead than alive. All the civil servants and officials talk of nothing but their departments and government offices; everything seems to have been crushed under a great weight, everyone is drowned by the trivial, meaningless labours which consume his useless life.

Gogol in a letter to his mother, 1829.

They will laugh at my bitter words.

The mis-quote from Jeremiah on Gogol's tombstone.

The heart of the matter and the main point about Gogol's 'advent into Russia,' is that Russia was, or at least appeared to be, a monumental, majestic and great power; yet Gogol walked over these real or imaginary 'monuments' with his thin, weak feet and crushed them all, so that not a trace of them remained.

V. Rozanov – a conservative contemporary critic.

Howard Colyer was born near Brixton Hill in London in 1961. His books include, *Oldshaw*, *Gregory Gun*, and a translation of Franz Kafka's, *Letter to my Father*. He has also written a number of plays including adaptations of Gogol's *Overcoat* and *Diary of a Madman*.

Marriage

Freely adapted from Gogol

Howard Colyer

Cover illustrations by Howard Colyer

Garamond 14 (v4)

ISBN 978-1-291-55925-5

Lulu.com North Carolina USA

Introduction

It was hissed off the stage. It wasn't understood. It failed. Gogol didn't attend the first night. Vsevolod Setchkarev gives this account in his biography:

The first performance in St. Petersburg took place on December 9, 1842; the first performance in Moscow, on February 5, 1843. The St. Petersburg performance was a complete failure and, in the opinion of Sergey Aksakov, the Moscow performance was also very weak. The reviews, with the exception of Belinsky's, who expressed himself very approvingly (for doubtful reasons, however) were almost entirely negative and devoid of any understanding. Neither the actors nor the critics, nor the majority of the public, were accustomed to this sort of comedy, and they simply did not know what to make of it. There was hardly any plot at all, the action developed very slowly...

Which made me think of the reaction to *Waiting for Godot* when it first appeared in London, and this sense of the similarity of the two plays has shaped my adaptation.

Just as Godot doesn't appear, nobody gets married in *Marriage*. At the end things are as they were in the beginning. There are events, but nothing happens. The waiting, hoping, scheming and the bursts of frantic activity have no consequence. And such is life. Such is life in the absurdist world view.

For Eric Bentley *Marriage* was a dramatic masterpiece equal to *The Government Inspector*. But even so *Marriage* has been overshadowed by Gogol's more famous work. *Marriage* is more purely absurd and the events are less eventful: at the finish Podkolyossin is still caught between his feeling that he should get married, and his fear of what this would entail; and Agatha is caught between her desire for marriage and the dreadful parade of potential husbands.

It could be said that this reflects the split in Gogol's own mind. His theme was insignificance. As a writer he portrayed a world where nothing was substantial and everything could pass away without a trace. But he became ever more zealous in his Christianity – and in his faith no act could be without significance; sin threatened everywhere; and the consequences were an everlasting afterlife either in Heaven or Hell.

Gogol was an absurdist who starved himself to death out of piety.

Hey ho!

Howard Colyer

13/08/2013

PS. In the original, Starikov – which translates as old man – makes a brief appearance. He says a couple of lines, lingers a while and exits. I agree with Eric Bentley that he's an off stage character who has wandered on to no good purpose.

PPS. I don't know Russian. I just wrestle with a dictionary.

Characters –

PODKOLYOSSIN, a bachelor and a court councillor.

STEPAN, Podkolyossin's servant.

KOTCHKAREV, Podkolyossin's married friend.

FEKLA, the matchmaker.

AGATHA, the woman being matched.

ARINA, Agatha's aunt.

DUNYASHKA, Arina's maid.

OMELETTE, a suitor – buys things for the government.

SHEVAKIN, another suitor – ex navy.

ANUCHKIN, a third suitor – ex drummer boy.

Podkolyossin's sitting room in which Podkolyossin sits with his pipe.

PODKOLYOSSIN:

Nothing to be done.

What else can be done?

Nothing else to do.

"A man who lives alone is a beast."

Socrates, he said it.

Said it right.

Or Plato?

Or Aristotle?

Did he say it?

No matter.

What's important is the beast.

A beast I am solitary.

So, a woman.

A woman's wanted.

A woman to be a wife.

My wife —

a woman.

What else can it be?

But a woman.

[He looks for Stepan.

Then shouts for him.]

Stepan!

Has that woman been yet?

[Enter Stepan.]

STEPAN:

Nobody.

No.

PODKOLYOSSIN:

The tailor?

STEPAN:

Nobody.

No.

PODKOLYOSSIN:

But you've been?

STEPAN:

Been?

PODKOLYOSSIN:

Been to the tailor's!

STEPAN:

    I've been.

PODKOLYOSSIN:

    And has he started?

STEPAN:

    After a fashion.

    He's doing the buttonholes.

    He starts there.

    Sign of a perfectionist –

    he said.

PODKOLYOSSIN:

    What?

    What are you saying?

STEPAN:

    Hole.

    Buttonhole.

    Hole for buttons.

    The beginning.

PODKOLYOSSIN:

    Did he ask why I need

    such a gentlemanly garment –

    a frockcoat?

STEPAN:

No.

Didn't ask me that.

PODKOLYOSSIN:

Perhaps he asked if I was

going to get married?

STEPAN:

No.

Nor that.

PODKOLYOSSIN:

No doubt you saw

all of the other frockcoats.

STEPAN:

Yes.

He's a tailor.

PODKOLYOSSIN:

Perhaps you noticed

the quality of mine.

STEPAN:

Sir, it has a quality.

PODKOLYOSSIN:

A superior quality.

STEPAN:

A quality all of its own.

PODKOLYOSSIN:

Did he remark how marvellous it was

in comparison to the others?

STEPAN:

No.

PODKOLYOSSIN:

Did he remark upon the

ultra fine cloth?

STEPAN:

No.

PODKOLYOSSIN:

Does he know my rank?

STEPAN:

Yes.

PODKOLYOSSIN:

Court Councillor!

STEPAN:

Yes, Sir –

that's your rank.

PODKOLYOSSIN:

My grade.

STEPAN:

Your grade.

PODKOLYOSSIN:

And it made him anxious?

STEPAN:

"We aim to please,"

he said.

PODKOLYOSSIN:

I bet he did!

Stepan, you can go.

[Exit Stepan.]

A black frockcoat!

Solid, respectable, reliable –

me!

Some men prefer to be bright –

to dress in gaudy colours.

I am not gaudy.

Gaudy Court Councillors get nowhere.

A Court Councillor is a Colonel.

Army – Colonel.

Civil Service –

Court Councillor.

The same!

I need envy a Colonel nothing

but his epaulettes.

Who said that?

Socrates?

Stepan!

[Enter Stepan.]

Boot polish –

you've bought it?

STEPAN:

I've bought it.

PODKOLYOSSIN:

Where did you buy it?

Did you go to that shop –

the one I mentioned –

on Voznessensky Avenue?

STEPAN:

That's where I went.

PODKOLYOSSIN:

And?

STEPAN:

>And I paid for the boot polish

>and I returned here.

PODKOLYOSSIN:

>First rate boot polish?

STEPAN:

>Sir, it's boot polish.

PODKOLYOSSIN:

>And you've tried it

>on my boots?

STEPAN:

>On your boots

>I've tried it.

PODKOLYOSSIN:

>And my boots gleam?

STEPAN:

>Nice shine, Sir.

PODKOLYOSSIN:

>And the shopkeeper –

>did he ask why your master needed

>wonderful polish?

STEPAN:

>Not a word on that.

PODKOLYOSSIN:

>Not curious?

STEPAN:

>Not that I noticed.

PODKOLYOSSIN:

>He didn't perhaps
>
>discuss my wedding plans?

STEPAN:

>No.

PODKOLYOSSIN:

>Very well, Stepan.
>
>*[Stepan exits.]*
>
>It's very simple –
>
>boots matter.
>
>So boot polish matters.
>
>Those who don't understand that
>
>don't get on.
>
>And polished boots
>
>are supple boots,
>
>and supple boots prevent corns,

and I hate corns on my toes.

Stepan!

[Enter Stepan.]

STEPAN:

You called?

PODKOLYOSSIN:

Did you say to the boot maker

that I can't stand corns?

STEPAN:

I said it.

PODKOLYOSSIN:

And what did he say?

STEPAN:

He said –

"Good!"

[Exit Stepan.]

PODKOLYOSSIN:

Busy, busy;

bustle, bustle –

so much to be done.

Getting married!

Easy to say;

hard to do.

Stepan!

[Enter Stepan.]

I want you to know...

STEPAN:

The old woman's here.

She coming down the path.

PODKOLYOSSIN:

The matchmaker?

STEPAN:

Her.

PODKOLYOSSIN:

Well, show her in!

[Exit Stepan.]

These things!

If not one thing –

the other thing.

Terrible things!

[Enter Fekla.]

Hello, hello, Fekla Ivanovna.

What's the news?

How's it going?

There's a chair.

Sit down.

Tell me all.

Speak, speak, speak, please!

FEKLA:

Agatha Tikhovna.

PODKOLYOSSIN:

Agatha!

Agatha?

Forty, I suppose.

Forty something.

More than forty?

FEKLA:

No, no, no, no —

never!

With such a wife

you'd be happier every day —

and every day

more grateful to me.

PODKOLYOSSIN:

Fekla Ivanovna —

if only you weren't such a liar.

FEKLA:

> Me!
>
> I hate liars like I hate a...
>
> bucket of stinking mackerel.
>
> Anyway –
>
> I'm too old for it now.

PODKOLYOSSIN:

> Dowry?
>
> Tell me of the dowry –
>
> truthfully.

FEKLA:

> I should say there's a dowry!
>
> A house made of bricks
>
> in Moscow –
>
> with a tenant in every room.
>
> The greengrocer's shop
>
> brings in 700 by itself.
>
> And there's a bar
>
> in the basement –
>
> thriving it is.
>
> Two extensions –
>
> one wood; one brick –

more rooms; more tenants.

There's the house in St. Petersburg –

which you'll see yourself.

And there's also an allotment

rented to a merchant –

allotment!

Small farm it is!

And he doesn't drink.

No!

No more.

"This dog's leaky in his liquor,"

he says.

Drink makes his tongue run away.

And he's got three sons –

two married already,

but the third…

PODKOLYOSSIN:

Enough!

Tell me about the woman –

this Agatha Tikhovna.

FEKLA:

What refinement!

What colouring!

So white –

a beautiful white neck.

As if her blood was made

of milk.

And sweetness!

Sweetness itself.

She is beyond words!

Words were not made for Agatha.

No!

I promise you –

you'll be grateful.

You will live your life

in gratitude.

"Fekla Ivanovna, thank you."

You will say over and over.

"Thank you."

PODKOLYOSSIN:

But she's no staff officer –

so to speak.

Not in the upper circle?

FEKLA:

> Her father was a merchant
>
> but her silk skirts rustle.
>
> She could be the daughter
>
> of a general –
>
> by her looks,
>
> her bearing,
>
> her everything.
>
> She said to me,
>
> "I don't mind a plain man,
>
> as long as his spirit is noble."
>
> You should see her on a Sunday!

PODKOLYOSSIN:

> Court Councillors need to be careful,
>
> you understand.

FEKLA:

> How could I not understand?
>
> You're not the first –
>
> we've had one already.
>
> A Court Councillor's come and gone.
>
> Looked nice, he did.
>
> But when he spoke –

one absurdity after another!

Each one more ludicrous

than the one before.

Man proposes;

God disposes –

he proposed;

she declined.

It obviously wasn't in God's plan.

And out he went –

down the road.

Down the road!

PODKOLYOSSIN:

Is there another woman

you want to discuss?

FEKLA:

Discuss!

Another woman?

We're contemplating –

contemplating Agatha Tikhovna.

There's none better.

PODKOLYOSSIN:

None better?

FEKLA:

Go seven times round the world –

you'll still find none better.

Try it –

if you don't believe me.

Go on!

I'll wait here.

PODKOLYOSSIN:

Thought –

careful thought, Fekla Ivanovna,

that's what it requires.

Come back –

the day after tomorrow.

FEKLA:

But we've been stuck like this

for three months.

You've sat on your sofa,

sucked on your pipe,

and seen one chance after another

vanish in the smoke.

PODKOLYOSSIN:

Three months is it?

FEKLA:

Three months!

PODKOLYOSSIN:

Until old age it lasts —

marriage.

Doesn't it?

Until old age!

What's three months?

FEKLA:

Enough to get somewhere

for those with a mind

to make the effort.

You want to get married

before you're old —

don't you?

PODKOLYOSSIN:

Well…

Yes.

FEKLA:

Then do something now.

PODKOLYOSSIN:

Now?

FEKLA:

>Coat and carriage –
>
>now.
>
>Go and see the lady
>
>before somebody else
>
>makes a proposal.
>
>Other men are on their way.

PODKOLYOSSIN:

>Other men?

FEKLA:

>Other men are moving –
>
>now.
>
>Moving through the city –
>
>on their way.
>
>Sit there and be left behind.
>
>Coat and carriage –
>
>that's all it takes.
>
>Get Stepan to drive you.
>
>Or take a cab.

PODKOLYOSSIN:

>What other men?

FEKLA:

> Other men with dark hair.
>
> They're not going grey.

PODKOLYOSSIN:

> Grey?
>
> Me?
>
> Where?

FEKLA:

> A captain, for example –
>
> a lancer.
>
> See him in his uniform
>
> and see a proper man.
>
> And a voice like a trombone.
>
> I'm keeping him in reserve.
>
> For if I mentioned Agatha
>
> he'd be riding –
>
> straight away.
>
> No delay there.

PODKOLYOSSIN:

> I must find a mirror.
>
> Stepan!
>
> My hair –

grey?

What next?

Smallpox?

[Exit Podkolyossin.]

FEKLA:

Why am I here?

Podkolyossin never moves.

He just dreams of action.

Could he talk to a woman

and propose?

Could he?

Could he do anything

but smoke a pipe

and cry out for Stepan?

[Enter Kotchkarev.]

KOTCHKAREV:

Podkolyossin, where are you?

You!

You here?

FEKLA:

As you can see.

KOTCHKAREV:

>The matchmaker who got me
>
>to marry a Devil.
>
>A Devil!

FEKLA:

>Are you having problems
>
>adjusting to each other?

KOTCHKAREV:

>Adjusting?
>
>Adjusting to Hell?

FEKLA:

>I'm sure Heaven is just
>
>around the corner.
>
>You only have to make a little
>
>allowance for peculiarities.

KOTCHKAREV:

>A little allowance…

FEKLA:

>For the women you wanted
>
>so much…

KOTCHKAREV:

>Because of your false description.

FEKLA:

A little colouring perhaps

around the edges.

Nothing more than that.

But still —

your friend's impressed.

KOTCHKAREV:

Podkolyossin?

You've started to help him?

FEKLA:

Three months ago.

KOTCHKAREV:

Three months!

He never said a word.

[Enter Podkolyossin with a mirror.

He sees only his own reflection.

Kotchkarev shouts.

The mirror is smashed.]

PODKOLYOSSIN:

Lunatic!

KOTCHKAREV:

Hypocrite!

PODKOLYOSSIN:

My mirror!

Hypocrite?

KOTCHKAREV:

Confirmed bachelor chasing skirt.

PODKOLYOSSIN:

Just an enquiry or two.

FEKLA:

Three months of discussion

and we've got nowhere –

I assure you.

KOTCHKAREV:

In everything the same.

PODKOLYOSSIN:

No, no, no, no –

no!

KOTCHKAREV:

Yes, yes, yes, yes –

yes!

Well?

Who is she?

PODKOLYOSSIN:

Just someone.

FEKLA:

Just someone?

Agatha Tikhovna!

KOTCHKAREV:

A neighbour?

PODKOLYOSSIN:

Not quite.

Round a couple of corners.

FEKLA:

Or three or four or five or six.

PODKOLYOSSIN:

Not six.

KOTCHKAREV:

Agatha Tikhovna Brandalistov?

FEKLA:

Agatha Tikhovna Kooperdyagin.

KOTCHKAREV:

Lives in Shop Street?

FEKLA:

Lives in Soap Street.

KOTCHKAREV:

The wooden house

before the stables?

FEKLA:

The brick house

beyond the tavern.

KOTCHKAREV:

Blonde?

FEKLA:

Dark.

KOTCHKAREV:

I know her well.

PODKOLYOSSIN:

You do?

KOTCHKAREV:

And marriage is a fine institution,

and a duty to God and Russia.

PODKOLYOSSIN:

Perhaps in the abstract.

But in the concrete —

or, at least, the flesh and blood…

KOTCHKAREV:

> The brick house
>
> just beyond the tavern?

FEKLA:

> The first one after the tavern
>
> houses a seamstress and
>
> a mistress of a senator.
>
> Then there's a sentry box.
>
> Then there's the house of
>
> Agatha Tikhovna Kooperdyagin.

PODKOLYOSSIN:

> Very interesting and perhaps one day…

KOTCHKAREV:

> Agatha Tikhovna Kooperdyagin?

FEKLA:

> Yes –
>
> Kooperdyagin.

KOTCHKAREV:

> Right!
>
> Out!

FEKLA:

> What do you mean –

out?

KOTCHKAREV:

You out of here

and out of this business.

PODKOLYOSSIN:

Kotchkarev?

KOTCHKAREV:

Off you go!

I'll handle this.

Second house after the tavern –

got that?

PODKOLYOSSIN:

I'm not sure there is any business.

FEKLA:

And if there is

it's a woman's business.

Matchmaking!

Always has been!

Swine!

Ingrate!

KOTCHKAREV:

You've told me all –

now clear out!

FEKLA:

Thief!

Atheist!

This is my living!

[Moves to the door.]

But let's see how it goes –

with him.

[Exit Fekla.]

KOTCHKAREV:

You heard her.

PODKOLYOSSIN:

Oh, yes.

KOTCHKAREV:

Well?

Defend yourself –

if you can.

PODKOLYOSSIN:

Perhaps she has a point.

KOTCHKAREV:

A point?

Look at this room.

What do you see?

PODKOLYOSSIN:

An armchair, a sofa, a table…

KOTCHKAREV:

No!

You see squalor –

the squalor of solitude;

the squalor of inertia.

PODKOLYOSSIN:

I thought it was rather comfortable,

but to a degree you might be right.

KOTCHKAREV:

A degree!

360 degress!

All round correct.

All round squalor.

And it must change.

Today.

This hour.

This minute.

This second!

PODKOLYOSSIN:

Oh, Kotchkarev, oh.

KOTCHKAREV:

While we wait she's dragging in

other men.

PODKOLYOSSIN:

Who?

Where?

False rumours.

KOTCHKAREV:

The matchmaker —

that Fekla —

she'll be dragging other men

to your Agatha.

PODKOLYOSSIN:

My Agatha?

KOTCHKAREV:

Yours!

If we act —

now.

PODKOLYOSSIN:

But what about my new boots?

I'm still waiting for those.

KOTCHKAREV:

Out!

On!

And up!

PODKOLYOSSIN:

As I am?

KOTCHKAREV:

As you are —

out!

PODKOLYOSSIN:

But I need a coat at least.

KOTCHKAREV:

Stepan!

[Enter Stepan.]

STEPAN:

Here.

PODKOLYOSSIN:

Coat.

STEPAN:

Frockcoat?

Here we go again.

PODKOLYOSSIN:

Overcoat.

[Exit Stepan.]

KOTCHKAREV:

Frockcoat?

Before the engagement?

PODKOLYOSSIN:

Well...

preparations...

you know.

KOTCHKAREV:

You prepare everything

except the one thing which is vital.

No woman; no marriage.

What's a frockcoat without that?

A thing for an idiot.

PODKOLYOSSIN:

Stepan might hear you.

KOTCHKAREV:

He knows, he knows.

[Enter Stepan with coat.]

STEPAN:

He does.

PODKOLYOSSIN:

What?

KOTCHKAREV:

Did you see where

that woman went?

STEPAN:

I saw how she went –

like a shot.

"I'll settle it," she said.

Over and over,

muttering hard,

racing along,

waving for a cab.

Then a cabbie stopped,

she dived in,

he cracked his whip,

the horse leaped –

off they flew.

KOTCHKAREV:

And so do we.

[Kotchkarev drags Podkolyossin outside
and looks for a cab as they talk.
Behind them the scene changes to Agatha's home –
and she and Arina are using a pack of
playing cards to tell their fortunes.]

PODKOLYOSSIN:

But it's strange,

terribly strange,

stranger than anything else.

KOTCHKAREV:

What?

PODKOLYOSSIN:

Don't you see?

KOTCHKAREV:

No.

PODKOLYOSSIN:

Marriage!

Being single;

not being single.

Transformation.

I'll be transformed.

I've never been transformed before.

So it's strange –

previously unknown.

And what about the wedding feast?

KOTCHKAREV:

Cab!

Podkolyossin!

Podkolyossin!

PODKOLYOSSIN:

Yes?

KOTCHKAREV:

But think of the joys.

PODKOLYOSSIN:

The joys?

KOTCHKAREV:

Imagine your wife's

little white hands.

PODKOLYOSSIN:

Well?

KOTCHKAREV:

Stroking your nose –

every night!

PODKOLYOSSIN:

>Every night?

>My nose?

KOTCHKAREV:

>Your nose –

>each and every night –

>stroke, stroke, stroke.

>Little white hands!

>And there'll be a budgerigar,

>or a parrot,

>in a cage.

>Your home will be a marvel –

>now a hovel,

>then a palace;

>or, so it will seem.

>And children…

PODKOLYOSSIN:

>Children!

>My papers –

>they'll mess them up.

KOTCHKAREV:

>Look at yourself.

PODKOLYOSSIN:

You broke my mirror.

KOTCHKAREV:

A solitary bureaucrat

without issue.

Cab!

PODKOLYOSSIN:

I can concentrate on my work.

KOTCHKAREV:

But if there were children…

PODKOLYOSSIN:

Yes?

KOTCHKAREV:

You'd have successors.

Men like you –

your children,

your children's children,

your children's children's children.

One Podkolyossin after another –

through all of the nineteenth century,

through the twentieth century,

through the twenty-first century –

they'll be men like you –

your descendants,

bureaucrats in your style –

until the end of time.

Your spirit,

your issue,

will pervade every office –

forever!

PODKOLYOSSIN:

Until the end of time?

Men like me!

KOTCHKAREV:

And I'll arrange the wedding feast.

PODKOLYOSSIN:

Yes!

KOTCHKAREV:

Cab!

[A cab stops and in they climb.]

AGATHA:

Again, my dear aunt, a journey.

And the King of Diamonds –

who might he prove to be?

And there's tears,

and a love letter,

and another gentleman –

the King of Clubs.

ARINA:

The King of Clubs!

A rival enters –

and his name is..?

AGATHA:

I don't know.

ARINA:

You do –

and so do I.

AGATHA:

Tell me.

ARINA:

A certain merchant

in the cloth business –

doing very nicely.

Alexsei Dimitrievich Starikov.

AGATHA:

Not him!

I don't think it's him.

Indeed I don't.

ARINA:

Don't be hasty.

The King of Clubs has black hair.

Straikov has black hair.

Therefore it must be him.

AGATHA:

Sorry, aunt, I'm not convinced.

A cloth merchant and a king –

how can that be?

They're opposites to me.

ARINA:

Agatha!

Think of your father.

How he'd hit the table

with his fists,

and threaten to spit at anyone

too proud to be a merchant.

'We're loyal Russians too,'

he'd shout.

'No colonel for my daughter,

and no son of mine

is joining the civil service!'

Those hands were as big

as buckets!

Mind you, your mother –

blessed woman –

would have lived a bit longer

if it hadn't been for him.

A terrible temper he had.

AGATHA:

Yes, exactly –

that's what I want to avoid.

ARINA:

Starikov's not like that.

AGATHA:

He's old!

And when he eats

he dribbles down his beard.

ARINA:

But can you do better?

AGATHA:

> Fekla Ivanovna –
>
> she's the woman to help.
>
> "A husband of the very highest quality
>
> and copper bottomed."

ARINA:

> Copper bottomed?

AGATHA:

> Copper bottomed, she said.

ARINA:

> Fekla Ivanovna is a terrible liar,
>
> so people say.
>
> *[Enter Dunyashka and Fekla.]*

FEKLA:

> Slander is a sin!
>
> A wicked sin.
>
> And that's the thanks I get
>
> for presenting people
>
> in their best light,
>
> and bringing together
>
> men and women.

ARINA:

Have you found someone?

FEKLA:

One!

I've found six.

AGATHA:

Six men!

FEKLA:

Six wonderful men –

incomparable.

But let me catch my breath.

[Dunyashka serves tea.]

I've run and I've run –

here, there and everywhere.

Like a woman possessed.

Where haven't I been!

Office after office;

house after house.

Army barracks –

I've stood outside a few!

Singing your praises –

enticing soldiers.

And that horrible old woman –

the one who married the Aferovs –

she almost attacked me.

"Get out of my district!"

That what she screamed.

Very territorial.

It didn't matter.

"For Agatha Tikhovna," I said,

"I'd venture down to Hell

and drag a man back from there.

If that's what needed to be done."

I'd fight with the Devil

for you, my dear.

And for my pains

I've managed to gather

the greatest choice of bridegrooms

in the history of the world –

in the history of the world!

And they're coming here today –

they're coming now!

AGATHA:

Six men now!

I'm not ready —

I'm unprepared.

FEKLA:

They're just coming

to give you the once over —

nothing strange there.

And you can have a look at them.

Very natural; very simple.

If you don't like them —

off they go!

ARINA:

All prime specimens no doubt —

deformed and deranged.

FEKLA:

Not deformed; not deranged —

specimens off the top shelf!

AGATHA:

Ooh!

FEKLA:

When shopping

it's best to have a choice.

[Exit Dunyashka.]

ARINA:

Gentlemen, are they?

FEKLA:

I've never seen such

gentlemanly gentlemen

in all my days of matchmaking.

Men and gentle

yet firm and strong.

AGATHA:

Aah!

ARINA:

Describe them then.

FEKLA:

Special reserve stock.

For example –

Balthazar Balthazavich Shevakin.

Naval officer, retired.

He likes flesh –

not a cannibal, I'm sure –

he's just adverse to

"a skeleton in a skirt,"

as he puts it.

But if you want

a very grand gentleman

then there's Ivan Pavlovich –

a civil servant, so important

it's barely possible to see him;

and round as well,

so when you do get to see him

you can't see past him.

Fills a door frame he does.

And he has a great booming voice.

"Cut the cackle –

no cackling here!"

That's what he roared at me.

"A woman's a woman,

tell me about her property

and movables."

And so I told him what you had

and he called me "a lying cow,"

then he used another expression –

which I won't repeat here –

but which revealed he was

a very important person indeed.

AGATHA:

And the others?

ARINA:

Any more,

"special reserve stock?"

AGATHA:

How old is he?

FEKLA:

How young is he?

He's a youth –

not a day over fifty.

AGATHA:

What's his surname?

FEKLA:

Omelette.

ARINA & AGATHA:

Omelette!

FEKLA:

Omelette –

an old and grand French family.

Here since the reign of

Catherine the Great.

AGATHA:

Then I'd be Mrs Omelette

if I married him.

Mrs Omelette!

No.

Never.

Better a spinster than that.

FEKLA:

Well, if the name's the thing,

then why not take

Balthazar Balthazavich Shevakin.

A good name and a good man –

an officer from the navy.

AGATHA:

What's his hair like?

FEKLA:

A fine head of hair –

like a lion.

AGATHA:

What's his nose like?

FEKLA:

His nose?

A wonderful nose –

like an eagle.

AGATHA:

Is he handsome?

FEKLA:

All his parts are…

just where they should be –

and all in the correct proportion.

But we all have our ways –

it takes all sorts to make a world –

and he's an avowed enemy

of furniture.

ARINA:

Enemy of furniture?

FEKLA:

Well, perhaps I've gone too far –

he doesn't have any, anyway.

Very little that I could see.

But he does have a stove.

AGATHA:

And the other men?

ARINA:

Equally special?

FEKLA:

Akinth Stepanovich Pantylev.

AGATHA:

Akinth?

ARINA:

A bureaucrat?

FEKLA:

Akinth, yes.

A civil servant, yes.

ARINA:

Akinth Stepanovich the drinker?

FEKLA:

He does have a reputation –

but I've seen him sober.

ARINA:

Next!

FEKLA:

Well –

there's one –

who I wasn't going to mention.

Not as sharp as the others.

And devoted to…

AGATHA:

What?

FEKLA:

Sitting on his sofa.

It's hard to get him to shift.

But a Court Councillor and

he prefers tea to alcohol.

Yes, a Court Councillor,

but I'm not sure what else he is.

AGATHA:

And the last one?

FEKLA:

You've had the lot already.

ARINA:

You said there were six.

FEKLA:

And you thought that was

overwhelming –

five's enough.

ARINA:

> Too many I think.
>
> Five gentlemen!
>
> One merchant is worth the lot!

AGATHA:

> I want a gentleman!

ARINA:

> Why?

FEKLA:

> Why?
>
> Because gentlemen count for more
>
> in the world.

ARINA:

> Picture Starikov —
>
> driving his sleigh
>
> along winter roads
>
> in that black coat of his —
>
> and his sable hat.

FEKLA:

> And then he'll meet a gentlemen
>
> with epaulets —
>
> and he shouts,

"Get out of the way

and take your hat off

and show some respect."

And then he'll want to see

some cloth and...

ARINA:

He won't show him any –

so the gentleman will go naked.

FEKLA:

Then out comes his sword.

ARINA:

Then he goes to the police.

FEKLA:

Then he goes to the Senator.

ARINA:

Then he goes to the Governor.

FEKLA:

Then the gentleman...

ARINA:

Is stuffed!

A Governor's more than a senator.

There's many a gentleman

who's eaten dust before

in Holy Russia –

believe you me.

[Enter Dunyashka.]

DUNYASHKA:

Excuse me, Madam,

a gentleman has arrived.

ARINA:

A gentleman!

FEKLA:

It's them –

or, at least, the first.

AGATHA:

It can't be!

FEKLA:

It is.

AGATHA:

I'm not dressed!

ARINA:

We're not tidy!

DUNYASHKA:

Shall I show him in?

ARINA:

Not yet!

[Arina and Dunyashka tidy the room.

Agatha looks out of the window.]

AGATHA:

I can see him.

He is fat!

Not just fat –

but fat!

FEKLA:

You mustn't keep him hanging about.

[Agatha runs out to get changed.

Arina runs after her.]

DUNYASHKA:

What shall I do with the gentleman?

FEKLA:

Bring him in!

Bring him in!

[Fekla hurries after Agatha and Arina.

Dunyashka goes down to the door.]

DUNYASHKA:

[Off stage.]

This way please, sir.

[Enter Dunyashka followed by Omelette.]

The ladies are just getting ready.

Excuse me, please.

[Exit Dunyashka.]

OMELETTE:

Wait must I?

Wonderful!

I just slipped out of the office

for a couple of minutes.

And if the general comes by?

And if he demands an explanation?

What do I say?

Sir, I was viewing a woman

as directed by a matchmaker.

And I know what he will say then!

But I'm here now —

so I won't turn about.

[He reads from a document.]

What's the inventory?

What's the reality?

Two storey stone house?

Checked!

Two wings –

one stone, one wood.

[Looks out of the window.]

The wooden one needs repair.

[Makes a note and

starts to examine the room.]

Furniture;

linen;

cutlery;

silverware…

[Dunyashka runs in from one door

and goes out of the other.]

DUNYASHKA:

Another gentleman!

OMELETTE:

What a bloody nuisance!

[Dunyashka returns with Anuchkin.]

DUNYASHKA:

Sir, please wait here.

They'll be down in a minute.

[Exit Dunyashka.]

OMELETTE:

My respects to you, sir.

ANUCHKIN:

And mine to you.

I'm so glad to meet

the head of the household.

OMELETTE:

Do you take me for him?

ANUCHKIN:

Aren't you her father?

OMELETTE:

I've fathered nobody!

ANUCHKIN:

Terribly sorry!

But you look paternal.

OMELETTE:

Bachelor.

And you?

ANUCHKIN:

Also a bachelor.

[Dunyashka runs through the room.]

OMELETTE:

Are you here...?

ANUCHKIN:

No, no, no, no!

OMELETTE:

Nor am I!

ANUCHKIN:

Just passing by...

OMELETTE:

Same here.

ANUCHKIN:

And here we are...

OMELETTE:

By chance.

ANUCHKIN:

Complete fluke.

[Enter Dunyashka with Shevakin.]

DUNYASHKA:

All the guests are waiting here, sir.

Please make yourself comfortable.

SHEVAKIN:

> You are a delight.
>
> Couldn't brush me down,
>
> could you?
>
> The dust about town these days!
>
> There's a speck there;
>
> and another there;
>
> and one there.
>
> And you must let me kiss you.
>
> Many thanks.
>
> And another kiss there;
>
> and…

DUNYASHKA:

> Stop!
>
> *[Exit Dunyashka.*
>
> *Shevakin goes to the mirror,*
>
> *admires himself and ruffles his hair.]*

SHEVAKIN:

> English cloth –
>
> lasts forever.
>
> Bought it in '95
>
> when the squadron was in Sicily.

Midshipmen then.

Made lieutenant 1801.

Sailed round the world in 1814.

The sleeves were a little frayed

at the cuffs.

Had them turned –

and the collar –

when I left the service.

Ten years now.

Almost as good as new.

OMELETTE:

Sicily?

SHEVAKIN:

Sicily in '95 for 34 days.

ANUCHKIN:

What language do they speak?

SHEVAKIN:

Not a word of Russian –

only French.

Throughout the island –

same everywhere.

The peasant with a bundle

on his back;

the lady on a balcony —

not a word of Russian.

But the ladies on the balconies

were exquisite —

even in French.

Brown they were

with ear rings everywhere —

not just in their ears!

Everywhere you could imagine —

and even places you couldn't imagine —

you'd find an ear ring.

ANUCHKIN:

They dressed with taste?

SHEVAKIN:

Extraordinary taste.

ANUCHKIN:

And they spoke French?

SHEVAKIN:

Nothing but.

OMELETTE:

Life in foreign parts

must be instructive.

With whom do I have the pleasure

of conversation?

SHEVAKIN:

Shevakin, sir.

Naval lieutenant, retired.

And yourself?

OMELETTE:

Civil servant by profession –

Omelette.

SHEVAKIN:

Thanks, but I've eaten already.

OMELETTE:

Omelette is my name.

SHEVAKIN:

Sorry!

Names, names, names!

And Russian names in particular.

In our squadron we had

a Tipsykov and a Topsykov.

You should have seen them scamper

when the wind picked up.

[Fekla enters and crosses the room.]

ANUCHKIN:

Morning, ma'am.

OMELETTE:

Good morning.

SHEVAKIN:

Good morning.

FEKLA:

Morning, morning, morning.

[Fekla exits and can be heard off stage.]

Try to be a man!

PODKOLYOSSIN:

[Off stage.]

I am.

KOTCHKAREV:

[Off stage.]

Try harder!

[Enter Fekla, Podkolyossin and Kotchkarev.]

What a gathering!

What a set of suitors.

[Gesticulations of denial.]

What we're lacking is a young lady.

FEKLA:

She's just getting dressed next door.

Not quite ready yet.

KOTCHKAREV:

Isn't she?

I think I'll just verify that.

[Looks through the keyhole.]

Lovely!

SHEVAKIN:

I'll check the report too.

Flesh!

ANUCHKIN:

I must check it too –

though it isn't altogether…

SHEVAKIN:

Look out –

somebody's coming!

[They hurry away from the door.

Enter Arina and Agatha.

The men all bow.]

ARINA:

And to what do we owe the pleasure,

dear sir?

OMELETTE:

Well…

My good lady…

Well…

Omelette's the name.

And I saw the advertisement

for the sale of timber,

and various departments need wood,

so I've come for the particulars.

ARINA:

The particulars –

for the sale of timber?

There's some mistake.

But now you're here,

please be seated.

SHEVAKIN:

I saw something

in the papers too.

Can't remember what it was –

but it's a lovely day,

isn't it?

ARINA:

And your name?

SHEVAKIN:

Balthazar Balthazavich Shevakin.

Former lieutenant in the navy,

now retired.

There was another Shevakin

in our squadron,

got hit just below the knee –

lower leg torn off,

just a bit of skin left

dangling down.

I'm not him –

not at all him.

Both legs complete,

and at your service.

ARINA:

Thank you.

Please sit there.

And you, sir?

Did you too see something

in a newspaper?

ANUCHKIN:

No, madam –

a neighbourly spirit

brought me here.

ARINA:

Are you the man

who's moved in opposite?

Into the house across the street?

ANUCHKIN:

No, I live in Peski.

ARINA:

But that's on the edge of town!

ANUCHKIN:

"Lord, who is my neighbour?"

Let us remember those words

from the Gospel.

Is not everyman my neighbour?

Indeed, indeed, indeed.

ARINA:

Neighbour, please sit down.

Sir, your reason please.

Is it our non-existent wood?

Or Christian fellowship?

Or are you perhaps

my long lost brother?

KOTCHKAREV:

Cousin actually!

ARINA:

You're my cousin?

KOTCHKAREV:

Second cousin –

to be precise.

But don't you recognise me?

And you, miss, surely?

ARINA & AGATHA:

No.

ARINA:

I've never set eyes on you –

as far as I know.

AGATHA:

Nor I –

not once.

KOTCHKAREV:

> Only once –
>
> but not long ago.
>
> Look again!

AGATHA:

> Was it at the Biryushkin's?

KOTCHKAREV:

> Exactly!
>
> At the Biryushkin's!

AGATHA:

> And you know what's happened
>
> to her?
>
> The daughter?

KOTCHKAREV:

> Got married?

AGATHA:

> Broke her leg.

KOTCHKAREV:

> I knew it was something like that.

AGATHA:

> The coachmen did it.

KOTCHKAREV:

Kicked her?

AGATHA:

Got drunk.

ARINA:

Clipped an iron post.

AGATHA:

Over they went.

ARINA:

Landed badly.

AGATHA:

In the street.

ARINA:

On the stones.

KOTCHKAREV:

I'll send her flowers.

AGATHA:

But I can't remember your name.

ARINA:

Please, remind us.

KOTCHKAREV:

Ilya Fomich Kotchkarev.

And this is my friend –

Ivan Kuzmich Podkolyossin.

PODKOLYOSSIN:

Very pleased to meet you.

ARINA & AGATHA:

Likewise I'm sure.

KOTCHKAREV:

Court Councillor Podkolyossin.

Not just a name,

but a by-word for efficiency,

for all those who know the civil service.

ARINA & AGATHA:

Podkolyossin –

a by-word for efficiency?

KOTCHKAREV:

That's right!

At this point he has a

special assignment –

something solo.

But within three days

he's sure to head

a section of his own.

His Director –

his immediate superior –

loves him so much

he even sleeps

in the same bed as him.

PODKOLYOSSIN:

What!

KOTCHKAREV:

Figuratively speaking –

sleep in the same bed.

Figure of speech.

Go figure –

as they say.

PODKOLYOSSIN:

Not actually…

No…

Not like that…

ARINA:

Gentlemen, please be seated.

[All are seated. Silence.]

OMELETTE:

Strange weather we're having.

This morning –

it looked like rain.

This afternoon –

it doesn't look like rain

AGATHA:

Very disturbing.

ARINA:

Unsettling.

FEKLA:

Worrying.

ANUCHKIN:

Bothersome.

SHEVAKIN:

Reminds me of Sicily.

We were there with the squadron,

my good ladies.

February I think it was,

but they called it spring.

The sun would shine,

and out you'd go.

The sun would stop shining,

and in you'd go –

before the rain.

First out;

then in.

All the time there –

in Sicily.

OMELETTE:

If you're married

in and out isn't so bad.

But if you're solitary,

it's dreadful.

ANUCHKIN:

Weighs you down.

FEKLA:

Makes you dull.

ARINA:

Makes you tired.

AGATHA:

It's torture.

KOTCHKAREV:

Terrible torture.

You wish you were dead.

God keep us all from such a fate.

[They cross themselves.

Silence.]

OMELETTE:

Might I ask…

Might I ask…

Might I ask, miss,

if you were married,

what kind of man

would he be?

What line of work…

would he follow.

Would he –

for example –

be the sort of man entrusted

to buy supplies

for the government?

SHEVAKIN:

Or would he be a man

with a naval background?

A man who had sailed

round the world

and seen South Africa

and India and China

and even taken an excursion

to Mongolia –

Inner Mongolia and Outer Mongolia –

even Outer Mongolia!

KOTCHKAREV:

No!

Think of a man

who can run a department

single handed –

and is well known to every minister.

ANUCHKIN:

But what about a man of culture?

A man who understands art –

but who's also served in the infantry?

Yes!

I was a drummer boy.

And we chased the French

out of Russia and back to Paris.

Drum, drum, drum,

and Napoleon –

run, run, run!

[Silence.]

OMELETTE:

Well…

Well, miss Agatha,

what do you say?

FEKLA:

Say something, dear.

AGATHA:

Aaaargh!

[Agatha runs out.

Arina and Fekla run after her.]

FEKLA:

[Off stage.]

But what will they think!

AGATHA:

[Off stage.]

Aaaargh!

[The door is slammed shut.

Silence.]

OMELETTE:

They've gone.

ANUCHKIN:

They have.

SHEVAKIN:

Something's up.

Probably something to do

with her dress.

Women's clothes!

Ha!

I remember in Sicily –

or was it Outer Mongolia?

Anyway…

[Enter Fekla.]

KOTCHKAREV:

Something is up, isn't it?

FEKLA:

Up!

I'll stick something up you!

You've made her ashamed.

You mustn't be so forward!

ANUCHKIN:

I thought I was rather backward –

if anything.

SHEVAKIN:

> Same here!
>
> 'Backward Shevakin' –
>
> that's what they called me.

OMELETTE:

> I know I'm backward.

FEKLA:

> But –
>
> she said if you return later
>
> she'll drink tea with you.
>
> But for now –
>
> be off!
>
> *[Exit Fekla.]*

OMELETTE:

> Drink tea later?
>
> Sounds like procrastination.
>
> Why don't we just get to the point?
>
> I'm a busy man –
>
> I can't spend all day getting married.
>
> This women has no sense of proportion –
>
> and no sense of time!

Tea today;

tea tomorrow –

then what?

Tea the day after?

KOTCHKAREV:

Not bad looking, is she?

PODKOLYOSSIN:

No, not bad.

Not bad at all.

SHEVAKIN:

Damn good looking –

I'd say!

KOTCHKAREV:

I'd thought her looks

would have been too domestic

– for you –

given your experience in exotic lands.

OMELETTE:

Her nose is too big.

ANUCHKIN:

Fine looks in my opinion –

and a lovely nose.

But what of her culture?

Can she speak French?

SHEVAKIN:

Try her.

ANUCHKIN:

How do you mean?

SHEVAKIN:

Ask her a question –

in French –

and she how she responds.

ANUCHKIN:

I can't speak French.

SHEVAKIN:

Then why do you care?

You could both

not speak French together.

ANUCHKIN:

But she's a woman.

PODKOLYOSSIN:

Very true!

ANUCHKIN:

If a woman doesn't know French –

is she really a woman?

OMELETTE:

But she has a fine house –

with two extensions.

Solid property.

Farewell.

[Exit Omelette.]

SHEVAKIN:

Time to smoke a pipe.

Are you going my way, sir?

Where is it you live again?

ANUCHKIN:

Petrovsky Lane in Piski.

SHEVAKIN:

Not quite my way,

but company's company.

ANUCHKIN & SHEVAKIN:

Good day.

[Exit Anuchkin and Shevakin.]

PODKOLYOSSIN:

And what are we waiting for?

KOTCHKAREV:

Don't you think she's sweet?

PODKOLYOSSIN:

More sour, I'd say.

KOTCHKAREV:

Five minutes ago

you said she wasn't bad looking.

PODKOLYOSSIN:

Her nose is too big,

and she can't speak French.

KOTCHKAREV:

Her nose is a delight –

I'd like to have it between my teeth.

And you don't speak French yourself.

In fact –

often you don't speak at all.

If you're going to be silent with her

one language is as good as another.

[Silence.]

Until the others started gabbling on

you were impressed.

[Silence.]

PODKOLYOSSIN:

I was.

I am.

KOTCHKAREV:

In that case –

let's do it!

PODKOLYOSSIN:

What?

KOTCHKAREV:

Close the deal!

The others have vanished –

so go in and propose.

Get yourself a wife.

PODKOLYOSSIN:

Now?

When she's so many suitors

to choose from?

KOTCHKAREV:

Look…

Okay –

I'll do it.

Just promise me you'll

stand by the agreement —

you won't vanish.

[Silence.]

PODKOLYOSSIN:

I promise.

KOTCHKAREV:

Shake.

[They do.]

PODKOLYOSSIN:

I need a smoke.

KOTCHKAREV:

Fine —

we'll have a pipe together,

then I'll come back in

and strike the bargain!

PODKOLYOSSIN:

Marriage it is!

[Exit Podkolyossin and Kotchkarev.

After a pause, enter Agatha.]

AGATHA:

This choosing business

is so difficult.

I haven't had many choices to make

so far.

Life has…

well…

rolled on…

so to speak.

Rolled on and dragged me with it.

Now I do have a choice –

and it's dreadful.

Fancy living in a world

where you had to make choices

all the time!

Terrible!

Terrible!

Terrible!

What madman could want that?

And I'm having to choose

without really knowing –

without understanding.

What are these men like?

What do I know of them?

What sort of man do I want?

I don't understand what's before me.

I don't understand my own needs.

But choose I must.

And there's four of them.

Four extraordinary men.

If only there were just two –

just two!

But which two?

Which one?

[Kotchkarev enters unseen.]

Omelette has substance.

Anuchkin has style.

Shevkin has seen the world.

And Podkolyossin?

He does have a nose!

A nose all of his own.

A nose a girl could face

across the breakfast table.

If only I could have it

in a little napkin.

A nose in a napkin!

[She stokes an imaginery nose in her napkin.]

Podkolyossin!

KOTCHKAREV:

Is the man for you!

AGATHA:

Aaargh!

KOTCHKAREV:

Podkolyossin is something –

the others are nothing.

Isn't it clear?

AGATHA:

Nothing?

KOTCHKAREV:

Shevakin –

nothing!

Anuchkin –

nothing!

Omelette –

the biggest nothing of them all!

He is zero to the highest degree.

AGATHA:

I didn't know you have

degrees of zero.

KOTCHKAREV:

If you married Omelette

you would find it was possible –

all too soon.

AGATHA:

Oh!

KOTCHKAREV:

Podkolyossin –

he towers above the rest.

He works miracles

in that office of his.

AGATHA:

Miracles?

What sort of miracles?

KOTCHKAREV:

One of his clerks died

and he brought him

back from the dead.

AGATHA:

Really?

I hadn't heard.

There was nothing in the papers.

KOTCHKAREV:

An adroit tap on the chest –

and everything was working again.

That clerk is now called Lazarus.

And Lazarus and Podkolyossin go about

arm in arm.

AGATHA:

But at least the others talk.

They don't visit in silence.

KOTCHKAREV:

Silent waters run deep.

He is contemplating the

administrative reform

of our entire Russian Empire;

he is considering a reply

to Kant's Critique of Pure Reason;

he is co-ordinating an expedition

to Patagonia.

AGATHA:

Patagonia?

KOTCHKAREV:

Patagonia!

AGATHA:

Where is Patagonia?

KOTCHKAREV:

Terra incognito.

AGATHA:

I hadn't realised.

KOTCHKAREV:

There you are –

marry Podkolyossin

and much will be revealed.

Secret avenues of knowledge

will spring open before you.

Life will be richer.

AGATHA:

So –

if I understand your drift –

you suggest your friend

as my husband.

KOTCHKAREV:

Yes, and he's waiting nearby –

in the café just down the street.

Let me go and fetch him.

AGATHA:

Podkolyossin?

KOTCHKAREV:

Podkolyossin forever!

AGATHA:

Yes, if I married him

I would be Podkolyossin forever.

But must I turn down the others?

KOTCHKAREV:

Polygamy is illegal.

AGATHA:

Must I really turn them down –

all of them?

KOTCHKAREV:

Yes.

AGATHA:

But how can I?

And I'd feel awkward.

KOTCHKAREV:

You just need to practise.

Turn one down

and the others will be easy.

AGATHA:

But what can I say?

KOTCHKAREV:

"Get out of my sight

you mangy dog!"

AGATHA:

Wouldn't that be rude?

KOTCHKAREV:

But it would work –

and the worst that could happen

is that he'd spit in your face.

AGATHA:

Spit in my…

KOTCHKAREV:

Face.

It happens.

Some of my best friends

have been spat on.

One fellow –

a good looking young man –

wanted a pay rise

so he pestered and pestered

his boss.

And eventually the man

could take it no more

and spat in his eye.

"There you are," he said,

"have a bonus instead of a rise."

But come pay day

my friend received

all the extra money he'd asked for.

It was worth the inconvenience

of a little saliva.

Russia is a marvellous country!

It would be different

if we didn't have handkerchiefs

to wipe our faces.

But you've got one there.

[Enter Dunyashka.]

DUNYASHKA:

Excuse me, miss,

you've another visitor –

Mr. Omelette.

Shall I show him in?

KOTCHKAREV:

It'd be better if he didn't see me.

Is there another way out?

AGATHA:

The backstairs are through there –

go straight ahead.

KOTCHKAREV:

I'll fetch your man;

you dismiss the riff-raff.

[Exit Kotchkarev.]

AGATHA:

Bring him in.

[Exit Dunyashka.]

Podkolyossin forever?

Is that my fate?

[She holds her handkerchief

in front of her face.

Enter Omelette.]

OMELETTE:

Are you about to sneeze?

AGATHA:

> *[She lowers her handkerchief.]*
>
> The urge has gone away.

OMELETTE:

> I'm sorry I'm early,
>
> but I'm early on purpose –
>
> I'm a purposeful man.
>
> *[Silence.]*

AGATHA:

> Well, Mr Omelette…
>
> What is your purpose?

OMELETTE:

> I have…
>
> I have a responsible position.
>
> I'm trusted by my superiors;
>
> obeyed by my inferiors;
>
> but…
>
> but…
>
> but I lack a wife.
>
> *[Silence.]*
>
> So, is it "yes" –

is that your answer?

AGATHA:

Did you ask a question?

OMELETTE:

I did!

AGATHA:

Did you just propose?

OMELETTE:

Wasn't it plain?

AGATHA:

I'm not thinking of marriage –

not just now.

OMELETTE:

What!

With matchmakers

flying here and there?

Matchmakers all over the place!

What's the meaning?

AGATHA:

Not now…

No…

Sorry…

OMELETTE:

Well!

[Enter Dunyashka.]

DUNYASHKA:

Two more guests, miss —

downstairs.

Oh!

They're here!

[Enter Shevakin and Anuchkin.

Exit Dunyashka.]

SHEVAKIN:

Hello!

ANUCHKIN:

Hello!

OMELETTE:

Good afternoon, to you.

AGATHA:

Thank you for coming by again —

so soon.

OMELETTE:

But our conversation wasn't finished.

What's the answer?

I have an appointment to keep.

AGATHA:

I gave you an answer.

OMELETTE:

Not one I'm willing to accept.

Do you realise who

you're dealing with?

Do you?

[Silence.]

AGATHA:

Mangy dog –

get out!

What have I said?

What have I said?

ANUCHKIN:

"Mangy dog" –

that's what it sounded like to me.

SHEVAKIN:

Oh yes –

I heard it too.

"Get out, you mangy dog –

out of my sight!"

A favourite expression

of the captain I served under

in the Mediterranean.

Never a day passed…

OMELETTE:

You said that to Omelette?

[He advances on Agatha.]

AGATHA:

He's going to hit me!

He's going to hit me!

[Arina and Dunyashka run in,

and look at Omelette in horror.]

ARINA:

He's gone mad!

DUNYASHKA:

Run!

Run!

Hide in the cupboard!

[Exit the women at speed.

Enter Kotchkarev.]

KOTCHKAREV:

Have I missed something?

OMELETTE:

>She had some sort of fit.
>
>Suddenly thought someone
>
>was going to hit her.
>
>Ran about screaming –
>
>then ran away.
>
>Somewhat strange I thought –
>
>and not a little troubling.
>
>Didn't seem to be all there.
>
>Relative aren't you?

KOTCHKAREV:

>Distant relative –
>
>second something or other –
>
>but still related.
>
>Why?

OMELETTE:

>Has it happened before?

ANUCHKIN:

>Is she excitable?

SHEVAKIN:

>Nervous?

KOTCHKAREV:

> According to her mother
>
> the attacks started three months
>
> before she was born.
>
> Frantic even in the womb!
>
> If you don't like highly strung women…
>
> then…
>
> Well!
>
> It does explain
>
> those exaggerated claims
>
> about property.
>
> Doesn't it?

OMELETTE:

> How do you mean?

KOTCHKAREV:

> Not altogether there –
>
> neither her nor the property.

OMELETTE:

> The property's not there?
>
> But we're standing in it.
>
> Explain.

ANUCHKIN:

> Do.

SHEVAKIN:

> Do.

KOTCHKAREV:

> Most of it is the bank's –
>
> or it will be when they finally
>
> give up the struggle
>
> to pay the mortgage.

ANUCHKIN & SHEVAKIN & OMELETTE:

> Mortgage!

KOTCHKAREV:

> 99% I believe –
>
> that sort of mortgage.

OMELETTE:

> 99%!
>
> That woman Fekla…
>
> *[Enter Fekla.]*

FEKLA:

> Good evening.
>
> Here I am.

OMELETTE:

> You disgusting fraud!
>
> Cheat!
>
> Liar!
>
> Out of my way!
>
> *[Exit Omelette.]*

KOTCHKAREV:

> A very excitable character –
>
> not altogether there.

ANUCHKIN:

> But what about French –
>
> are the claims true?
>
> I must know.

FEKLA:

> What is going on?

KOTCHKAREV:

> The claims of French?

FEKLA:

> Tell me.

ANUCHKIN:

> She claimed she could
>
> speak French.

FEKLA:

It's true.

KOTCHKAREV:

It's false.

SHEVAKIN:

They speak French in India,

you know.

FEKLA:

She's fluent.

SHEVAKIN:

Speak French in China too.

KOTCHKAREV:

Doesn't know a word.

SHEVAKIN:

They even speak French

in Outer Mongolia –

not a word of Russian.

ANUCHKIN:

So, if we went to Outer Mongolia

we'd be lost.

Good day!

[Exit Anuchkin.]

FEKLA:

Where's Agatha?

KOTCHKAREV:

Locked herself in a cupboard –

I believe.

All thanks to your matchmaking.

[Exit Fekla.]

SHEVAKIN:

Lucky you're here then.

KOTCHKAREV:

How do you mean?

SHEVAKIN:

Being related.

KOTCHKAREV:

Yes?

SHEVAKIN:

Being related…

You could put a word in –

for me.

KOTCHKAREV:

With Agatha?

SHEVAKIN:

I think she's very attractive.

KOTCHKAREV:

My dear sir –

do you own a mirror?

SHEVAKIN:

I do.

KOTCHKAREV:

And do you think

you're equally attractive?

SHEVAKIN:

I'm still a fine figure of a man.

KOTCHKAREV:

But your hair is grey.

Your beard is grey.

And your grey suit looks like –

you've been round the world in it.

SHEVAKIN:

I have!

KOTCHKAREV:

A long time ago.

SHEVAKIN:

Not too long.

KOTCHKAREV:

Get yourself to a barber's.

Get yourself to a tailor's.

Get your hair blacked,

your beard trimmed,

and buy some new clothes –

bright, cheerful, youthful, fashionable.

Make yourself like a peacock –

return here –

and I'll say something in Agatha's ear.

SHEVAKIN:

Right!

Like a peacock.

Okay!

Thank you for your

Words of wisdom

I'll be back in a week.

KOTCHKAREV:

That's the spirit.

[They shake hands.]

SHEVAKIN:

Friend!

KOTCHKAREV:

Friend!

[They embrace.]

SHEVAKIN:

Farewell!

KOTCHKAREV:

Farewell!

[Exit Shevakin.

Enter Agatha.]

AGATHA:

Mr Shevakin?

Mr Anuchkin?

Have they left as well?

KOTCHKAREV:

Arm in arm –

I believe they've fallen in love

with each other.

AGATHA:

With each other?

KOTCHKAREV:

> They've set off to drink
>
> to male friendship.
>
> They'll be at it all night.
>
> Drunken debauchery
>
> is their favourite past-time –
>
> often ending in bouts of arson.
>
> Fire raisers –
>
> fire starters.
>
> Read of a fire in the morning –
>
> and you'll know the origin.

AGATHA:

> I never guessed.

KOTCHKAREV:

> They confided in me.

AGATHA:

> Lucky you came.

KOTCHKAREV:

> Especially as I can vouch
>
> for one good man.

AGATHA:

> Your friend?

KOTCHKAREV:

> Yes –
>
> but he should be here
>
> by now.
>
> One moment.
>
> *[Kotchkarev opens the door*
>
> *leading down to the main entrance.]*
>
> Why are you standing there?

PODKOLYOSSIN:

> Couldn't seem to get over
>
> the threshold.

KOTCHKAREV:

> In!
>
> At last –
>
> together.
>
> I need to send a message –
>
> one more instruction
>
> to the caterers.
>
> So I'll leave you alone –
>
> for a little while.
>
> *[Exit Kotchkarev.*
>
> *Silence.]*

PODKOLYOSSIN:

    Miss Agatha…

AGATHA:

    Yes?

PODKOLYOSSIN:

    Do you…

    like boats –

    rowing boats?

AGATHA:

    Well…

    somewhat.

PODKOLYOSSIN:

    I like rowing in a boat –

    in summer.

AGATHA:

    Yes, in summer

    a boat can be nice.

PODKOLYOSSIN:

    But you never know

    what the weather

    is going to do –

    even in summer.

AGATHA:

    Our Russian weather!

    But still –

    a nice day in summer

    is very nice.

PODKOLYOSSIN:

    It is.

    [Silence.]

    Miss Agatha…

AGATHA:

    Yes.

PODKOLYOSSIN:

    Do you…

    like flowers?

AGATHA:

    Oh, yes –

    I like flowers.

    Flowers with a scent.

PODKOLYOSSIN:

    So do I.

    [Silence.]

    Miss Agatha…

AGATHA:

Yes.

PODKOLYOSSIN:

Church?

AGATHA:

What about church?

PODKOLYOSSIN:

Church –

last Sunday?

Did you go to church?

AGATHA:

I did.

PODKOLYOSSIN:

So did I.

The Kazan Cathedral.

And you?

AGATHA:

The Church of the Ascension.

PODKOLYOSSIN:

But what I always say is,

whatever church you go to,

God is always the same.

Don't you say that as well?

AGATHA:

Those very words –

indeed.

[Silence.]

PODKOLYOSSIN:

Miss…

Speaking is when silence

at last falls silent.

AGATHA:

What?

PODKOLYOSSIN:

Socrates, I think.

We can only silence silence

by speaking…

But…

Oh dear…

I'd better be going now.

AGATHA:

So soon?

PODKOLYOSSIN:

They say all good things

come to an end.

And…

And…

I'm boring you.

AGATHA:

No!

Not at all.

We're having such a

delightful conversation.

Thrilling!

PODKOLYOSSIN:

No, no.

AGATHA:

Yes, yes.

PODKOLYOSSIN:

So…

May I come again?

AGATHA:

As often as you like.

PODKOLYOSSIN:

Thank you.

[Exit Podkolyossin.]

AGATHA:

> Well!
>
> What a man!
>
> Extraordinary!
>
> And such a deep thinker.
>
> His face reveals it all —
>
> the hours of contemplation.
>
> Doesn't talk much —
>
> that's true.
>
> But nor do I.
>
> But I'm sure we'll have some
>
> marvellous silences together.
>
> Being silent with him
>
> will be so much better
>
> than being silent by myself.
>
> I must tell my aunt!
>
> *[Exit Agatha.*
>
> *Enter Kotchkarev dragging Podkolyossin.]*

KOTCHKAREV:

> Why are you going home?

PODKOLYOSSIN:

> We've had our talk.

KOTCHKAREV:

> You've proposed?

PODKOLYOSSIN:

> Not...
>
> directly...
>
> but...

KOTCHKAREV:

> Is she going to marry you?

PODKOLYOSSIN:

> Well...
>
> probably...
>
> at some point...

KOTCHKAREV:

> Good.
>
> The ceremony occurs
>
> in an hour.

PODKOLYOSSIN:

> What!

KOTCHKAREV:

> Don't delay –
>
> you're a Russian.
>
> Hurl yourself on!

What are consequences to you?

PODKOLYOSSIN:

But…

today?

KOTCHKAREV:

You said you'd be ready

once the others

were out of the way.

I've cleared the field –

so, keep your word.

PODKOLYOSSIN:

Naturally, I can –

and I will.

But I'm not used to…

keeping it so quickly.

Let's pause for…

six weeks, say.

KOTCHKAREV:

The caterers are prepared;

the witnesses are prepared;

the priests are prepared.

PODKOLYOSSIN:

Oh, God!

KOTCHKAREV:

He is prepared as well.

PODKOLYOSSIN:

Sorry –

I wish I could.

But…

KOTCHKAREV:

You can;

you must;

you will.

What about if I kneel?

[He does.]

What about if I kick you?

[He does.]

PODKOLYOSSIN:

Aaargh!

No!

Stop!

It's no good.

Not today.

I can't.

Why are you so intent

on doing this?

KOTCHKAREV:

I want to transform you.

Rouse you.

Wake you up.

You are Russia!

PODKOLYOSSIN:

No, I'm not.

I'm Podkolyossin.

Russia's over there –

out of the window,

down the street.

KOTCHKAREV:

I must get you

off your couch.

PODKOLYOSSIN:

I like it there.

KOTCHKAREV:

But you do nothing –

always nothing.

PODKOLYOSSIN:

>I dream a little.

>*[Kotchkarev slumps.]*

KOTCHKAREV:

>Go, go, go!

>I wash my hands of you.

PODKOLYOSSIN:

>Do you?

KOTCHKAREV:

>Yes.

PODKOLYOSSIN:

>What a relief!

>Well…

>good-bye.

>*[Exit Podkolyossin.]*

KOTCHKAREV:

>I hope you break your neck

>in a traffic accident.

>Drunken cabbie.

>Gruesome collision.

>Torso pierced by the shaft.

>Limbs scattered everywhere.

Head on a spike.

You obliterated.

[Silence.]

No…

Don't do it.

Don't give up.

Russia must be saved!

[Kotchkarev flies after his friend.

Enter Agatha.]

AGATHA:

Podkolyossin –

my fate!

Wherever I turn

I see him –

his image is implanted

in my mind's eye.

And I hear his voice

in my ear.

So this is the prelude

to marriage.

When we are married

I will truly

see him everywhere,

and hear him everywhere –

if he speaks.

Farewell my single life.

I'm to be married –

then what troubles will come?

Children!

Boys –

will they be drunks?

Will they be gamblers?

Girls –

will they marry drunks;

even drunken gamblers?

Everything will be lost

on a turn of a card.

I can see it now!

Oh, my children!

The house and everything –

lost!

[A sob.]

But it hasn't happened –

not yet.

No!

And I'm only twenty-seven

and I haven't had much fun.

[Silence.]

But where is he?

[Pokolyossin is flung through the door

by Kotchkarev.]

PODKOLYOSSIN:

Miss Agatha…

I've returned to discuss

one small point.

AGATHA:

And what point is that?

PODKOLYOSSIN:

Very small point –

detail actually.

[Silence.]

So –

what do you say?

AGATHA:

Say to what?

PODKOLYOSSIN:

   To the point at question.

AGATHA:

   You haven't said…

PODKOLYOSSIN:

   Not precisely…

   But…

   Between us…

   There might be a doubt…

   a doubt or two…

   three perhaps.

   Yet…

   We could…

   Talk some more…

KOTCHKAREV:

   Will you marry him?

PODKOLYOSSIN:

   Hold on!

AGATHA:

   Yes –

   I consent.

KOTCHKAREV:

>And I bless this union.

>Oh, happy couple.

>Now –

>kiss!

>*[Thy do after a fashion.]*

>Well –

>there'll be more time later.

>An hour later –

>when you're married.

AGATHA:

>An hour!

>Is that what you said?

KOTCHKAREV:

>I've done the lot.

>Everything is ready.

>Everyone's prepared.

>But where's your dress?

AGATHA:

>It's in my bedroom.

KOTCHKAREV:

>Well –

put it on.

Get changed.

Get ready.

And I'll send word

of your imminent arrival.

[Exit Agatha.

Exit Kotchkarev.]

PODKOLYOSSIN:

Marriage!

Who would have thought?

Marriage to Agatha.

A woman.

I can tell.

As I said before,

and Socrates before me,

a man who lives alone

lives like a beast.

Office, home.

Home, office.

Traipsing forth and back.

Barren –

infinitely barren.

If I were the Tsar

I'd order everybody

to get married in an hour

or have their heads cut off!

Or, at least,

that's what Kotchkarev said.

But –

marriage doesn't mean

only happiness lies ahead.

But –

you've bound yourself now.

And it's immediate.

And it's irreversible.

But –

you're not actually married.

Not yet.

But –

you're betrothed.

A priest is preparing the altar.

Preparing the sacrifice.

But –

I can't go down the stairs.

He'll get me –

drag me back.

And there's a maid

guarding the rear door –

I'm certain.

But –

The window!

There's a tree!

It will break my fall –

and if it doesn't,

I'll escape a fate

worse than death.

[Podkolyossin leaps.

Off stage –

a branch breaks;

a man falls to the ground;

a cry is heard,

"Cabby, quick, Semyonlovsky Bridge."

A cab drives away.

Enter Agatha, Fekla and Arina.]

FEKLA:

Congratulations.

I must admit

I had my doubts

as to your intentions.

ARINA:

You're a lucky man

to have such a bride.

AGATHA:

Where is he?

ARINA:

Dunyashka!

[Enter Dunyashka.]

DUNYASHKA:

Yes, madam.

ARINA:

Did Mr Podkolyossin

slip out the back?

DUNYASHKA:

No, madam –

he jumped out the window.

AGATHA & FEKLA & ARINA:

What!

No!

It's too high!

DUNYASHKA:

I saw him fly

through the air.

[Enter Kotchkarev.]

KOTCHKAREV:

All ready then?

FEKLA:

No –

your man's scarpered.

KOTCHKAREV:

How?

The doors were covered.

FEKLA:

The window was open.

A fine match you've made.

KOTCHKAREV:

He had the gumption

to jump out of a window?

FEKLA:

To escape your plan –

you meddler!

KOTCHKAREV:

Who saw him jump?

DUNYASHKA:

I did.

He broke a branch

off the tree

on his way down.

Hailed a cab

and shouted out,

"Semyonovsky Bridge."

KOTCHKAREV:

Right!

I shall return –

with Russia in my hands.

And Russia shall be

redeemed!

[Kotchkarev leaps.

Off stage –

a branch breaks;

a man falls to the ground;

a cry is heard,

"Cabby, quick, Semyonlovsky Bridge."]

ARINA:

Gone.

AGATHA:

And my husband too.

DUNYASHKA:

The same way.

FEKLA:

When the bridegroom

jumps out of the window,

the marriage flies

over the rooftops –

old matchmakers' proverb.

AGATHA:

No!

ARINA:

But there's still Starikov.

Perhaps he'll come tomorrow.

Waiting for him isn't so bad.

He'll come tomorrow –

without fail.

*** *Curtains* ***